The Fight

Elizabeth Karre

SURVIVING SOUTHSIDE

The Fight

Elizabeth Karre

darbycreek
MINNEAPOLIS

Darby Creek
A division of Lerner Publishing Group, Inc.
241 First Avenue North
Minneapolis, MN 55401 U.S.A.

Website address: www.lernerbooks.com

The images in this book are used with the permission of: © Bellurget
Jean Louis/StockImage/Getty Images, (main image) front cover;
© iStockphoto.com/Jill Fromer, (banner background) front cover
and throughout interior; © iStockphoto.com/Naphtalina, (brick wall
background) front cover and throughout interior.

Main body text set in Janson Text LT Std 55 Roman 12/17.5.
Typeface provided by Adobe Systems.

Library of Congress Cataloging-in-Publication Data

Karre, Elizabeth.
    The fight / by Elizabeth Karre.
        p.   cm. — (Surviving Southside)
    ISBN 978–1–4677–0596–7 (lib. bdg. : alk. paper)
    [1. Toleration—Fiction. 2. Sexual orientation—Fiction.
3. Gay-straight alliances in schools—Fiction. 4. High schools—
Fiction. 5. Schools—Fiction. 6. Hispanic Americans—Fiction.]
I. Title.
PZ7.K1497Fi 2013
[Fic]—dc23   2012025132

Manufactured in the United States of America
1 – BP – 12/31/12

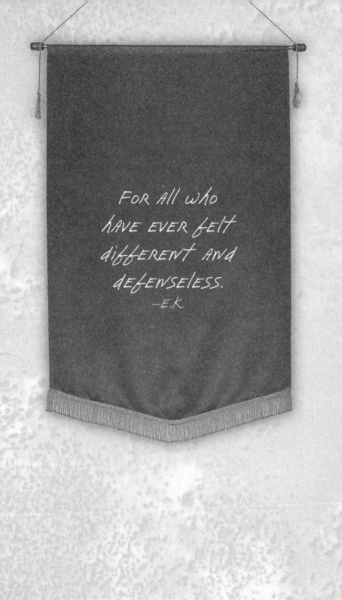

FOR All who
have ever felt
different and
defenseless.
—E.K.

CHAPTER 1

"**F**aggot."
    I heard the word at the same time I heard the clang of metal. I was coming around the corner, rushing to get to English before the bell. I saw Jay pushing someone against a locker.

"Faggot, bet you like it," he said and reached down, I think, to grab the guy's crotch. I gasped. Jay looked at me, and I saw that it was Dominic he was on.

"Bet you want some too," Jay said to me. Then Ms. Weller stepped out of the classroom, about to close the door. My brain wasn't moving fast enough to even understand what was happening.

"Everybody, get to class," Ms. Weller said sharply. "The bell's about to ring." She jerked her head toward the classroom for me. The bell made its horrible noise. I obeyed without thinking. My eyes stayed on Dominic, crumpled against the locker.

I totally expected Ms. Weller to step out into the hall and deal with Jay. I thought that "get to class" was for me. Like for confidentiality reasons or whatever it is that teachers are always trying to get rid of everyone else when someone's getting in trouble.

But she followed me into the classroom. The door shut behind her. Dominic and Jay were alone in the hall.

My feet kept moving to my desk in the front row. I slid into my seat. I couldn't believe it. It must have showed on my face.

"What's wrong?" my friend Jenny whispered, leaning across the aisle.

"Take out your papers and pass them to the front," Ms. Weller said from her desk. "We're starting a new unit today."

I shook my head at Jenny, *not now*. I dug into my bag looking for my paper. My hands were shaking.

Jenny kept staring at me. She mimed writing and raised her eyebrows. I held up a finger. Lester poked me in the back with a stack of papers. I took them and added mine. Ms. Weller was striding along the front of the classroom, picking up the stacks.

"Thank you, Isabel," she said as I handed her the stack. I could tell she was trying for a normal voice. I didn't think I could look at her. At the last minute we locked eyes. It took my breath away like always—she had the most beautiful eyes ever. At the same time, I couldn't read her expression.

As Ms. Weller started talking about our new unit, Harlem Renaissance poetry, I wrote a note to Jenny. I told her what had happened in the hall. I told her how Weller did *NOTHING*.

"Remember how she was all over that guy who called Keesha the n-word during passing time?" I wrote. "Weller took him to the office. He got suspended! But she just LEFT Dominic in the hall with that a-hole. I'm worried about him. :(It was really scary." I tossed the note on Jenny's desk.

"RU sure she saw/heard it?" Jenny wrote back.

"She had to see it, and I'm sure she heard him say FAGGOT. She was RITE THERE!" I scribbled.

Jenny thought a minute before writing back.

"Im sorry, Bella. Sucks. Specially since you love Wellie so much. Dom's prolly ok, though," I read.

"I hate this school," I wrote back. "I can't wait to be done with Southside High FOREVER."

CHAPTER 2

When I got home from school, my brother Matteo was home for the weekend. Probably more to see his friends than us, his family.

"Kids cook!" my mom announced. "I'm going to yoga. Use that half an onion in the fridge and whatever else you want. Let's eat at six. Papi and I will both be home then."

Matteo shook his head. "I come to see you all from working so hard at college, and all

I want is a good home-cooked meal. . . ." He pretended to wipe away tears.

"Whatever," I said. "I still have to cook on 'kids night,' but I'm doing all the work alone now. So start chopping. You're doing dishes too."

While we worked, Matteo talked, like always. He was always a pretty nice big brother to me. Sure maybe it was only because I'd spent my entire life hanging on his every word and thinking he was perfect. But this time, after Matteo ranted about some political stuff and raved about his philosophy class, he actually asked me how school was going.

I didn't know how to answer. I was still upset about Dominic, but I wasn't quite ready to talk about it.

Without waiting for an answer, Matteo said, "What are you reading in English? It's too bad you don't have Watson. She was so cool."

"Umm, I think we're starting the Harlem Renaissance next," I said.

I didn't mind not having Ms. Watson. She looked like a guy, and she talked in this abrupt way. Not like the beautiful Weller, who wore the most amazing clothes. I loved staring at her in class. Anyway, Watson had left Southside after Matteo graduated.

"Cool—I took a whole class on the Harlem Renaissance last year, remember?"

I stared at him blankly.

Matteo laughed. "Izzy, you so don't even listen to me."

"Don't call me Izzy," I said automatically.

After dinner, I unpacked my backpack. I wasn't going to start any homework on a Friday night, though. Matteo grabbed my reading list for English. He frowned.

"Didn't you say you were doing the Harlem Renaissance? How come Langston Hughes isn't on this list?"

I shrugged. I was looking at my math assignment and wondering if I should try to do it when Matteo was around so he could help me.

"When are you going—" I started.

"And James Baldwin? Countee Cullen? Claude McKay? What the . . . "

I yanked the list out of his hands. "Matteo, I don't *know*. I don't know who any of those people are. And I don't care right now. And neither did you when you were a junior in high school. Even if you are super smart."

I could feel tears coming into my eyes. I didn't even know what I was fighting about with him. "I just had a stressful day, OK?" I muttered, shoving the list in my folder.

But Matteo was barely listening to me. "I think some or maybe all of those guys were gay," he said. "I remember because that unit was how Watson kind of came out to us. I mean, most people already thought she was, but she was pretty open about discrimination back then and what she'd experienced."

He had my attention now.

"Those guys you said were gay? And none of them are on the list?"

What the hell, I thought, too. Was Weller some kind of gay hater? Did that explain her actions today? For some reason, this made my stomach plunge.

"Umm, Matteo? Did kids beat up other kids for being gay when you were at Southside?"

He looked at me. "Yeah, sometimes.

I never saw it, but I heard rumors. Certain teachers were super strict about kids saying 'that's so gay' and stuff. Watson, obviously. And Salazar—he's gay too."

"Salazar's gay?" I said. He taught theater, not a class I'd had.

"Yeah," Matteo shrugged. "So what?"

"So what? So what? It's like in your little liberal college bubble you've forgotten what it's like where we live. It's a big deal at Southside if people just think you're gay!" I was getting worked up.

"Whoa, what's up?" Matteo asked. Then his phone rang. "Oh, sorry, I gotta get this," he said and turned away as he answered. "Hello?"

"Hey, Matt," I heard a girl's voice say.

"Hey, Casey, what's up?" he said, walking out of the living room. I heard the door to his room shut. I put my head down on the table.

CHAPTER 3

On Monday I had a plan. I was nervous about it. I had kind of thought before about joining our school's gay-straight alliance, the GSA, as everyone called it. I needed more extracurriculars for applying to colleges next year anyway, and the GSA probably wouldn't involve a ton of work or meetings.

The GSA was new at Southside, I thought. There had been some big deal about it last year, but I hadn't really paid attention to it. I mean, when I first heard about it, I didn't think it had anything to do with me. And these seniors, Carmen and Scott, who had been in charge of it or something were kind of scary. Carmen rolled her eyes at me in the bathroom once because I was putting on lipstick.

But now I thought I should check it out. Maybe I'd see Dominic there. I could see if he was OK. We used to be friends, kind of. Our families went to the same church. During confirmation a couple of years ago, our moms had carpooled sometimes. And we'd just ended up hanging out during the class (which could be pretty boring). We knew each other from school, and neither of us knew the other kids very well. But we didn't have any classes together this year so I hadn't seen him much.

And seeing Matteo always reminded me that I should do more extracurriculars and work harder in class. He, of course, had done everything in high school from sports to theater. And he got good grades. I was less stellar. I didn't want to worry about scholarships and stuff yet, but my mom was starting to drop little hints.

I had barely seen Matteo the rest of the weekend. He had been out with his friends or in his room talking or texting or something to that Casey girl. And I have a life, of course, too.

So checking out the GSA was just my idea. I was kind of proud of it—and nervous.

I thought I remembered posters about the GSA meetings, so all morning I kept scanning the hallway walls. Nothing. Well, lots of other stuff like the next dance, tryouts for whatever, blah-blah.

So at lunch I tried to ask my friends about the GSA casually.

"I think it was shut down," said Kim. "Or didn't, like, start. Wasn't that guy, the cute senior, trying to start it or something? Is he gay? I thought he had a girlfriend."

The others shrugged. I guess, like me, they hadn't paid much attention because it didn't seem like something for us. We all liked guys, not girls. So for the rest of lunch, we just talked about who were the cutest boys in our grade.

CHAPTER 4

It was a regular week. I couldn't remember all the writers Matteo said were gay, but I don't think Ms. Weller mentioned any of them. But I liked some of the stuff we were reading.

My friends were trying to set me up with this guy, José. He and his friends ate lunch with us sometimes, but he didn't seem too interested in me. I thought he was nice but not much more than that. I'd had a boyfriend at the end of last year, but he graduated. It seemed stupid to try to keep dating while he was in college, and I had two years of high school still.

But I missed the attention. And making out. We seriously kissed for hours straight. Or it felt that way. It was pretty awesome. Even though he was older than me, he never pressured me. And we didn't really date long enough for a lot to happen. So I had some experience but not enough to ever feel like I really knew what to do around guys or how to make one like me.

Keesha and I were walking to health class on Thursday when we passed José at his locker. Keesha nudged me and called out, "Hiiiiii, José. Whasup?"

He just nodded at us.

After we'd passed him, Keesha smacked my arm. "Did you even smile at him? Girl, we can't do all the work for you, you know!"

I shrugged. "I don't think he's interested. And he's nice but—" I broke off because June was approaching the classroom just as we were. My stomach flipped over, and I could feel my face get super hot.

"Hey," she said locking eyes with me (because I was staring at her) as she walked past me through the door. I watched as she tossed her long hair out of the way to slide her bag off her shoulder as she sat down. I sighed.

"Why are you blushing?" Keesha said, interrupting my thoughts. She followed my gaze. "Is that why you're not interested in José?" she asked, her eyebrows raised.

I blushed even harder and hurried to my desk. I wasn't even sure what she meant exactly.

CHAPTER 5

After school everyone was going their separate ways to activities or jobs. Lots of times Jenny gave me a ride home, but I could walk home too. I didn't want any of my friends with me today because I wanted to walk by the theater and Mr. Salazar's classroom and see if there were GSA posters there. Now that Matteo had told me Mr. Salazar was gay, I thought I remembered that he was the teacher adviser for the GSA back when people were talking about it.

There wasn't anything by the theater or the school office. I thought Salazar's classroom was on the first floor too, so I kept walking, peeking into classrooms as I passed. The custodian was following me down the hall, rolling a really loud trash can, and it was making me nervous. My hands were sweating.

I could hear kids talking in a room up the hall. I tried to see in as I walked by slowly. I saw Salazar right away. He was really cute, but he definitely looked gay. I wondered why I hadn't really noticed before.

It didn't look like a meeting to me. I was so busy looking at them as I walked by that I hadn't looked at his door to see if he had a poster on it. I stopped to look at another poster like I was reading it (just in case the custodian was watching). Then I slowly turned around and walked back to pass Salazar's room again.

I heard one of the girls say, "And then she's all like 'Eww, that's so gay. He's so faggy.'" Salazar's response was too quiet for me to hear, but all the kids started laughing. I slowed down and fumbled around in my bag like I was looking for something. I came to a stop outside his classroom, trying to listen.

I snuck a look up at the door. No GSA poster or anything. I glanced inside again. Salazar looked right at me and smiled.

A girl came up to him and looked at me too. "Who's that?" she said. It was the girl who'd been talking earlier.

I gave them a weak smile and a wave like, *don't mind me*, and hurried down the hall.

CHAPTER 6

O ut in the parking lot I breathed a sigh of relief to be out of that awkwardness. But then I immediately felt annoyed and stupid. Maybe I should have just asked him. But I wasn't totally sure he was the adviser. There should be some place you could look up all the extracurriculars and their advisers. I was walking fast now, feeling mad.

But why did I care anyway? I should just sign up for the yearbook or something if I really wanted an extracurricular.

A squeal of tires at the end of the parking lot made me look up. A guy was walking far ahead of me and a car was driving next to him, swerving and braking hard. At first I thought it was guys just messing around with a friend or trying to talk to someone.

Then I recognized the backpack was Dominic's. He was walking with his head down as a guy hung out the window, yelling something at him.

I held my breath as the car squealed again as it turned hard away from him. Good, they were leaving.

Then I saw they were just turning around to come by him again. I thought for a second that they were going to drive up on the sidewalk and hit him or something crazy like that. Dominic jumped over onto the grass. They braked hard again, the whole car rocking. Everyone in the car was screaming something, and then all this trash came flying out the windows. A bottle was going right toward Dominic's head. He ducked. I think I might have yelled, but you wouldn't have heard it because the car roared off then.

I was too far to run and catch up with Dominic, especially with my schoolbag.

"Dominic!" I yelled. He didn't turn around, but I thought he heard me because he turned his head a little and hunched his shoulders. Maybe he thought I was another person trying to hurt him.

Our houses were the same direction from school, so I jogged behind him, breathing hard. I lost some time at the busy street by school because I had to wait forever to cross. By then he'd disappeared into the neighborhood.

When I got into the neighborhood myself, I couldn't see him ahead of me. The straightest way to his house was the street I was looking down, but he wasn't there. I kept glancing up the other streets as I walked by, but I never saw him.

CHAPTER 7

Then it was Sunday. I was sitting in church with my mom, worrying about all my homework. Sundays suck like that.

My dad didn't come to church often. It was weird because my mom had converted to Catholicism when they got married. He didn't ask her to or care about it, but sometimes it seemed like she was trying to out-Latino him to prove she wasn't really white. She spoke Spanish to us way more than he did and wanted all our teachers and friends to call us by our full names, pronounced exactly right.

I also think my name—Isabel—sounds better in Spanish, so I just told most people to call me Bella, instead. Izzy is a stupid name, so I hated it when people tried to call me that.

My mom was kneeling and praying before the service. She was looking a little too devout. I wished I had Matteo there to roll my eyes at. I was flipping through the program thing they give you with all the songs and announcements.

Since there weren't any guys I cared about at church, I was wearing the kind of dressy clothes my mom liked. "Classy" she called them. Nothing that showed bra straps and "nice" shoes that matched my skirt. I drew the line at nylons, though.

While I was waiting for the service to start, I thought about how in every class and even in my lunch period there was a cute guy that I could keep an eye out for. Someone who made me care about how I looked just in case he saw me. Some of them didn't know I existed. Like the senior at lunch who was on the soccer team and always polished his apple on the waistband of his boxer shorts.

I started ticking through them all. English: Andre. Math: David. History: Ricky. Health. . . . Maybe because there weren't any interesting guys in health, I spent so much time looking at June's profile and long, shiny hair. But I didn't like her the way I liked those guys, did I? The things my body did when I saw her—blushing, clammy hands, pounding heart—it was how I felt with cute guys too.

Looking down at the part in my mom's hair as she bowed her head, I flashed on a memory from a long time ago. I had asked her what a lesbian was. She explained and then seeing something in my face, she said, "Oh, but I know you're not a lesbian, honey."

"How do you know?" I asked. (Good question because I was, like, eight!)

"You like boys too much," she said.

I turned my thoughts away as the choir started the first song and my mom pulled me to my feet.

CHAPTER 8

When I got a little bored during the sermon, I started reading the announcements again. Deaths, births. And this:

Join us next week at noon on Wednesday for the archbishop's prayer service for the sanctity of marriage—marriage between one man and one woman.

I elbowed my mom. She pulled her eyes off the priest and gave me an annoyed look. I pointed to the announcement in the program.

She glanced at it and frowned.

"Later," she hissed and turned her face back to the priest.

I was annoyed right back at her. Maybe it didn't seem like the laws around gay marriage mattered to how kids were treated in school, but it just seemed mean.

When everyone came forward for Holy Communion, I saw Dominic there with his family. I couldn't catch his eye. When the service was over, I told my mom we had to go have donuts at fellowship time. She raised her eyebrows but followed me.

First, I only saw Dominic's parents with his siblings. Then I saw him over by the wall, not talking to anyone. I grabbed a donut and said to my mom, "I'm gonna go talk to Dominic . . . about something at school. A . . . a project." I'm not sure why I lied.

As I hurried over, I realized I had no idea what to say. Sorry you're getting beat up 'cause you're gay? Does our school have a GSA? I'm not gay, I'm just curious—about the GSA, not other stuff?!

He didn't look up as I approached.

"Hey," I said, standing in front of him.

He looked up through his bangs. "Oh, hi," he said softly.

"Good donut?" I blurted out. Wow, that was stupid.

He shrugged.

"Umm," I said. "I just wanted to know if you were OK. I mean after Jay . . . "

Dominic blushed and looked really uncomfortable. "Uh, yeah, I'm fine," he said.

"I couldn't believe Ms. Weller didn't take him to the office," I said, feeling mad at Weller all over again.

Dominic shrugged. "Not a big deal," he mumbled. Now I was getting annoyed with him.

"No, it was," I insisted. "And I saw those guys throw stuff at you from the car. It was scary." I looked hard at his face, trying to make him look at me.

When he finally did look at me, the pain in his eyes made like an ESP connection between us.

"They've done other stuff too, haven't

they?" I asked. "What did they do? Who is it? Jay?"

He shifted and looked away again. "I don't want to talk about it," he said in a soft voice.

"Have you told on them?" I asked, squeezing my donut until it started to make crumbs. All kinds of scary pictures were going through my head of what a bully like Jay might do to Dominic.

He shrugged again. "You saw what happened with Weller. I did try to talk to the vice principal once. He just told me to try to stay out of their way. And maybe not act so . . ." He trailed off.

I squeezed my donut so hard a chunk broke off and fell on the carpet. Not to act so gay is what the vice principal said, I could tell. I knew what he meant, but what did that even mean?!

I don't know if I'd ever consciously thought about Dominic being gay until I heard Jay call him a faggot, but it totally made sense. I had known Dominic since junior high, and he'd never been like other guys. It didn't matter, but now I was pretty sure he was.

But the vice principal saying "Well, son, just try not to be so gay" (I could hear him saying it, the tool) was stupid. It was just how Dominic was. And why should he have to change for an idiot like Jay who was always trying to feel girls up in the hall and crap like that.

"What about your parents? Can't they talk to the principal?" My mom would be calling everyone from the superintendent on down if she thought me or Matteo was being harassed at school.

Dominic looked panicked. "No, and don't say anything. You can't tell your mom or anything. They don't know. . . . They don't know."

I guessed what he meant is that they didn't know he was gay. I guess his parents were kind of conservative and traditional. But still . . .

"Can't you just tell them that Jay and those guys are bugging you and won't stop? Just so someone tells them to leave you alone or something. Or they should totally get suspended for throwing a bottle at you. I can say I saw it."

Dominic was shaking his head the whole time. "No, no. I can't tell my parents. They're—they're under a lot of stress right now."

He stopped. I raised my eyebrows.

"Our house is getting foreclosed," he added reluctantly.

"Oh, wow," I said, stupidly.

"Besides," he said quickly, "It wouldn't make any difference anyway with those guys. They don't care about getting in trouble. They'll . . . they'll stop soon," he said, unconvincingly.

I didn't know what to say. I felt so bad for him. Then our moms both came over and said that it was time to go and that it was nice to see each other again. I mumbled to Dominic, "I'll see you in school."

On the way home, my mom said, "What were you showing me in the announcements?"

"Nothing," I said and put my head back and closed my eyes.

CHAPTER 9

I t took me a while to realize on Monday that there was something going on. I didn't really notice the T-shirts until third period. I was sitting behind Rachel, reading over and over again on her back: LET'S TALK! THE BIBLE HAS THINGS TO SAY ABOUT MARRIAGE.

I remembered I had seen similar shirts on kids in the halls, all with the same logo.

After class I asked her, "What's up with your shirt?"

"Oh, hey, Bella!" she said, all perky. "I thought your church participated. It's a day to spread the Bible's message about love and marriage and how God cares for everyone's soul. And that our actions, even when we're young and maybe confused, really matter." She stared at me earnestly.

I just shook my head and walked away.

━━ ━━ ━━ ━━ ━━

I threw myself down at our lunch table. "You will not believe what Rachel said to me," I told my friends.

"She's wearing one of those T-shirts, right?" said Kim. "Someone else gave me a card on my way here, but I didn't read it." She pulled it out of her back pocket. I grabbed it.

"Oh my God, listen to this," I said. "'The Lord has our best interests at heart when it comes to our sexuality.'" I threw the card down. "You know what that means—God hates gay people and so do we!"

Jenny and Keesha exchanged looks. Kim picked up the card to read it.

"You don't think the Bible says being gay is bad?" asked Keesha.

I stared at her. "I don't know what the Bible says about it. Or about a lot of other stuff. But this is BS! Why, do you think that?"

Keesha put her hands up. "Whoa, I didn't say that. I'm just saying that for some people who are really religious, it's just obvious. You should hear my grandma talk about it."

I shook my head as I picked up my milk.

"Why are you so upset?" asked Jenny. "You didn't used to care so much about . . . political stuff." She paused. "Is this about Dominic?"

"What about Dominic?" Keesha and Kim said. I gave Jenny a look.

"Jay was . . . harassing him the other day and calling him terrible things," I said. "And Ms. Weller didn't do anything."

Keesha shuddered. "I hate Jay," she said. "He's always got to be messing with somebody." Kim nodded. Then she moved on.

"Hey, did you guys hear about—"

I tuned Kim out. I wasn't in the mood for gossip about other people's love lives.

CHAPTER 10

A fter school I decided just to go out the door by Salazar's room. No good reason. When I came to that hallway, it was like déjà vu. Dominic was backed up against the lockers. But this time it was two of those kids in the stupid T-shirts. And they weren't grabbing him, but they were in his face.

"—seen how you look at guys in the locker room," the guy was saying to Dominic. "You know it's wrong, unnatural."

"It's only because we care that we don't want to see you go to hell." The girl put a hand on Dominic's arm. He flinched.

"You can change," the guy said. "There are camps that can help—"

"Shut up!" I yelled, striding toward them. "Leave him alone!"

The girl faced me. "We're just talking. It's a private conversation."

"Well, I'm ending your conversation," I spat, reaching out to pull Dominic away from the guy.

That girl I'd seen in Salazar's room before came out in the hall with her hands on her hips. Not letting go of Dominic, I started walking toward her. I just felt we'd be safer down there. The T-shirt kids whispered together and then went the other way.

"What's going on?" the girl asked as we got up to her.

"Those stupid—" I couldn't even think what I wanted to call them.

"Homophobes," she said, nodding. "A bunch of the churches do this every year.

Disgusting. Are you OK?" she asked Dominic.

He looked as if he was trying not to cry. He shrugged and whispered, "Yeah."

"You guys want to come in? Salazar lets us just hang out in his room. I'm Zoe, by the way."

I totally wanted to, but Dominic shook his head. "I told my mom I'd be home to babysit."

"You walking?" I asked. He nodded. "I am too so we can go together." He didn't look too excited. "We'll see you later," I said to Zoe. I definitely wanted to talk to her again.

First, we were quiet as we walked, but I couldn't hold back long.

"You don't really think that, do you? That you're going to hell?" I asked.

Dominic shrugged—it was like his answer to everything. "It's in the Bible," he said finally.

"But so is tons of other stuff no one takes literally!" I said. "Like remember when we learned the Ten Commandments, and it says you can't take the Lord's name in vain. Everyone does that, it's not a big deal."

"This is different . . . worse," he said, sadly.

"But that guy saying you could change," I

said. "That's total BS. Why should you try to change? There's nothing wrong with you."

Dominic just kept his head down.

Suddenly I remembered that guy in school, Jamie Ballard, who had killed himself last year. I didn't know him, but the rumors were that he was bullied. I felt really scared. Maybe I should tell someone. But Dominic asked me not to.

"Umm, so what are you doing tonight?" I asked.

"Just babysitting," he said. "My dad doesn't get home till eight. Homework."

"You wanna do something this weekend?" I asked. I just felt that I needed to keep track of him. "I mean, you could just come over and we could watch a movie or something."

"Maybe," he mumbled. "I'm gonna turn here. . . ." It was blocks before he needed to turn, but I guessed he'd rather cut through the alleys than keep walking with me. Still, I got his number. Later, I texted him so he'd have my number, but he didn't reply.

CHAPTER 11

When I got home, my mom was there. I wanted to tell her so bad. What I had seen wasn't good, and I could just tell worse stuff had happened to Dominic. It seemed crazy that no adults were helping him. But I remembered what he'd said about his parents. I couldn't tell my mom without involving them too.

The next couple of days, I walked past Dominic's locker a lot just to see if he was OK. I said hi a few times.

I had decided I was going to make him do something on the weekend. I didn't want it to seem like he was just my pity project. I was trying to think who else I should invite to hang out too. It would be more fun with someone else since Dominic wasn't the best company. And then it wouldn't be heavy like all we did was talk about him getting bullied. We could just have fun like normal people.

By Thursday I'd decided to ask Kim to hang out with us. Then I'd find Dominic in school or text him or call him if I didn't see him.

Kim said sure if it was after seven on Saturday because she had to work. But I couldn't find Dominic.

I hurried home to call him.

My mom doesn't let me take my phone to school. No one's supposed to ever take their phones out at school, of course, but everyone does constantly, including the teachers. They can't ban phones completely because lots of parents are worried about a school shooting or something. Apparently not my mom. She also barely lets me use it after dinner because she says that's "family and homework time."

When I got home, I had a text from Dominic from a couple of hours earlier.

":(," it said.

I sent him three texts.

"What's wrong?"

"Were you in school?"

"Lets make plans 4 weekend. Sat nite good?"

I waited impatiently, flipping through channels on the TV, holding my phone in my lap. After ten minutes I called.

No answer.

Five minutes later. I called again and left a message.

I texted him again.

"RU OK?"

"CALL ME!"

I was feeling totally panicked. I tried to calm down.

Maybe he was sick, and that's what the sad face meant. Maybe he was taking a nap right now. Maybe he left his phone at home when he went somewhere. Maybe it was off. Out of battery. Maybe he shared it with his parents. Or they stopped paying the bill (no, he just texted me, I thought). Maybe he dropped it in the toilet. Maybe he was just sick. . . .

I paced in the kitchen until my parents got home.

"How was school?" Mom asked. Then she frowned. "Didn't you see my note? Why didn't you get the stuff out of the freezer for dinner or turn on the oven?"

I mumbled an apology. Now I saw the note. I had been in the kitchen for over an hour without noticing it.

My mom raced around huffing. She filled a large pot with hot water and threw the chicken in to defrost. My dad rubbed his belly.

"Oh, oh, I'm so hungry. My daughter wants me to die of starvation." His eyes twinkled at me. I couldn't even summon a smile. My mom pursed her lips.

"I have to leave again in forty minutes for a meeting. You might have to eat without me." She sniffed.

I just wanted to ask my parents if everything was OK and have them say yes. With my mom in a bad mood, though, I didn't want to start.

Everything is fine—everything is fine, I told myself.

"Isabel!" my mom snapped. "Could you make the salad? I'm going to just have a sandwich. You'll need to watch the chicken. Papi has some work he needs to do tonight."

After Mom left, I tried to numb my brain with the radio while I finished making dinner. I called Papi to eat.

"Wow, you set the table!" he said, giving me a squeeze. "I thought that was my job tonight since you were cooking."

I smiled weakly. We talked a little at dinner. A couple of times I felt Papi looking at me like he was going to ask if I was OK. I just kept my eyes down.

Papi said he'd clean up, so I fled to my room. I'd had my phone in my pocket the whole time, so I knew I hadn't gotten any calls or texts, but I still had to check.

I called and texted Dominic again just

because I couldn't help it. Then I thought of something.

My dad was singing along loudly with the radio in the kitchen.

"Papi, do you know the Garcias' phone number?"

"The Garcias?" He looked confused.

"From church," I said. "Their son Dominic is my age, you know?"

He wiggled his eyebrows at me. "Ooh, their son Dominic . . ." I just shook my head at him. "No, but you can look in the church directory."

I was already going through the junk drawer.

I went to my room to call, keeping my fingers crossed. It rang and rang. Finally, an old-school-sounding answering machine picked up with a message in Spanish. I hung up.

Then I called back and left a message in Spanish and English.

Now there was nothing left to do except keep my phone close. It was a good thing my mom was gone tonight. I knew she wouldn't remember my phone by the time she got home.

I was in my pajamas and trying to read Zora Neale Hurston for English when Mom came in.

"You're in bed?" she said. I could tell she felt bad about being mad earlier.

"Yeah, just really tired. I'm going to bed after I finish this assignment," I said.

"I'm exhausted too," she said, yawning. "I'm going to take a shower and go to bed. Good night, sweetie." She gave me a long hug, and I almost started crying. Maybe I should tell her right now. Then she yawned another huge yawn. "I'll send Papi in to say good night."

As I lay in the dark, I held the phone in my hand, sometimes staring at the screen. I fell asleep with it under my cheek.

CHAPTER 12

I woke up to a phone ringing. I groped in my bed, but then I heard my mom in her room.

"Hello? . . . No, no! Oh my God, ohhhh . . ." Her voice died off into murmurs. I felt frozen in bed. Then I forced myself to get up and go in my parents' room.

My mom and dad had their arms around each other, and my mom was crying. As soon as she saw me, she grabbed me hard and pulled me against her. My dad put his arms around both of us and put his face in my hair.

"What? What?" I was trying to say. There was a huge knot in my stomach.

My mom pulled away to look at me.

"Dominic Garcia died yesterday. He killed himself."

CHAPTER 13

My mom said I could stay home, but I went to school anyway. I felt like I had to somehow.

I ended up telling my parents everything because my dad remembered that I was trying to call Dominic last night. Then, because it didn't matter anymore, I told them he was gay, being bullied.

"Being bullied? That's terrible," my mom said. We were all sitting in a row on my parents' bed. They seemed to want me near them. "Did he tell anyone?"

I went into the whole thing, and I could see my mom getting ticked off. "An administrator *said* that?"

Papi patted her arm. "Stay calm." I could tell Papi was a little freaked by the gay angle. Then we all had to get ready to go.

I didn't see any of my friends before homeroom. I wasn't sure if I was going to burst into tears or what when I did see them.

I had my head down on my desk when the morning announcements came on.

"We've had a tragic loss," the principal's voice said. "Dominic Garcia, a junior here at Southside, died yesterday from self-inflicted injuries. Out of respect for his family and confidentiality, we cannot give you any more details. Our thoughts and prayers are with Dominic's friends and family. Grief counselors available today for any student who needs to talk to someone. Again, please keep Dominic's family in your prayers."

And that was it.

CHAPTER 14

The rest of the day was a blur. When I did see my friends, they were nice, but they wanted to know the details. I hadn't wanted to ask my mom about how Dominic did it, and she hadn't told me. So I didn't know any more than anyone else. And it didn't matter—however he'd done it, Dominic was dead.

At lunch, people were buzzing about it. Some of Jay's friends were laughing loudly at their table. I stared at them with hate.

As I was throwing my stuff away, Zoe came up to me. She looked as sad as I felt.

"Hey," she said. "Dominic Garcia—that was your friend, right?"

I hesitated. I wasn't sure "friends" is how I'd describe me and Dominic. But I nodded.

"I'm really sorry," she said seriously. She took a deep breath. "I thought you might be interested—we're going ahead and meeting even though we don't have approval yet. I thought you might want to come."

"To—?" I said.

"The GSA meeting. Tomorrow after school in the courtyard. Salazar said he can't let use his room." Her mouth twisted. "If you know anyone else who might be interested, pass it on. But be careful." She tossed her stuff and walked away.

"Who was that?" Jenny asked as she came up.

"Oh, just somebody I know," I said.

Both my parents came home early just to sit with their arms around me again it seemed. Not that I minded. They talked a lot about feelings and seeking help and resources.

Finally, I interrupted.

"I've never thought about killing myself. Really."

"Do you promise you won't?" my dad whispered.

"I promise," I said.

Then we all started to cry.

After a while my mom wanted to hear again about the bullying and what Dominic had tried to do about it.

"That really needs to be looked into," she declared. "We don't know exactly why Dominic . . . ended his life, but that kind of harassment can't be ignored by the adults in a school."

"I know," I said. "And usually they do *something*. But Mom, Dominic's parents don't know and you can't tell them. They didn't know he was gay. And I don't think this is the time for them to find out."

"Are you sure he was . . ." Papi trailed off.

"*Gay*, Papi, it's not a bad word," I said, annoyed. "I don't know, but he never denied it to me and it seems like he was."

Papi screwed up his face, thinking. I could see he was trying to remember who Dominic was and whether he looked gay. Whatever. I turned back to my mom.

"Who would you talk to anyway? And what would you say?" I didn't want her going out there making things even harder.

She shook her head. "You're right. I'm not sure. But that other boy last year? who also . . . took his life—didn't it come out later that he was bullied too? Something about Facebook?"

I nodded. I didn't really know anything else about it, though.

She pulled me closer. "I just worry there are more kids out there going through that and no one's helping them," she said.

Me too.

CHAPTER 15

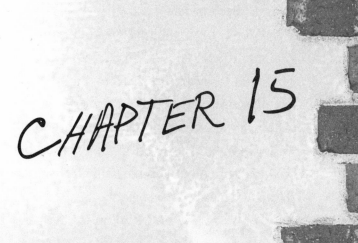

I didn't want to be the first one at the meeting, so I hung around my locker the next day after school. Jenny offered me a ride home and looked at me funny when I didn't give a good reason for turning her down.

Finally, I walked slowly down to the doors by the courtyard and saw Zoe and some other kids sitting at a picnic table.

Zoe nodded to me as I sat down. The other kids looked at me in surprise. They all seemed to know each other.

"I don't think you told me your name," Zoe said to me.

"Bella," I cleared my throat. "I'm Bella."

"Dominic was her friend," Zoe told the others. Some of them looked sympathetic. Zoe went around the table telling me names, but I couldn't remember any of them after she said them. My hands were sweaty.

"Umm, excuse me," said one of the guys. "Emma, or whatever your name is—"

"Bella," I said softly.

"Uh-huh—but are you gay?"

I sucked in a huge breath, and my entire body felt flushed dark red. Before I could stutter an answer, Zoe jumped in.

"Oh my God!—Tyler!" she screeched. "I can't believe you'd ask that. Do you not know what GSA stands for? Gay Straight Alliance! It doesn't matter whether someone's gay or straight or just doesn't want to tell you." She glared at him. He shrugged.

"We need to be careful who we trust with our secrets. I don't know her. I don't know who this Dominic kid is—was—either. What does he have to do with us?"

"Dominic was gay and being harassed because of it," Zoe hissed. I was surprised—how did she know? "Right?" she turned to me.

I hesitated, then nodded. "I mean, he never told me he was gay but . . ." I paused. I didn't want to offend anyone here. They were all pretty . . . obvious. Like kind of stereotypical gay guys or lesbians. Zoe was wearing cargo shorts, and Tyler was wearing eyeliner.

I wasn't sure what secrets Tyler was talking about because it didn't seem like a secret that he was gay or trying to look gay. Dominic hadn't been anything like that.

"He was *gender nonconforming*, which means he didn't act or look like some pigs thought a guy should," said Zoe.

"How did you know he was being bullied?" I asked her.

"I saw a few things," she said briefly, giving me a look like *later*. She looked at the door. "I thought a few other people were coming, but this might be it." She seemed disappointed that it was only six of us.

"OK, *boss*," said Tyler. "What's the plan?"

"Well, I thought we'd just go around and say why we wanted to be here or have a GSA at our school," said Zoe. My stomach dropped. Somehow I had thought I could just sit back and listen. A couple other kids had similar uncomfortable looks on their faces.

"Some of you know that last year a couple of students did all the paperwork and got all the signatures, but the principal still hasn't approved the GSA," Zoe continued. "That's why Salazar can't be here and we can't meet in his room. So if we're going to keep fighting to be acknowledged, we need to know why."

She looked around. "Fine, I'll start. I want a GSA so everyone who's gay or questioning knows they're not alone. And because they can't put us back in the closet!" She punched a fist in the air. The girl next to her threw an arm around her and kissed her on the cheek. Her girlfriend, I wondered?

"Amen," said Tyler sarcastically. "I want a GSA so I can find some hot boys at this school to date. Other than you, Emilio," he added, patting the short boy next to him. "You're a little young for me." Emilio blushed.

"I want . . ." Emilio trailed off. "I just want a place to talk about . . . being . . ." he sighed.

"Gay," said Tyler for him.

"I can't tell my family. They just . . ." he shot a look at me. Zoe nodded.

"Lots of people aren't out to their families . . . yet," she said.

Emilio squirmed. I could see him thinking he'd never be able to tell. That's how Dominic felt.

Then everyone was looking at me. "Uh," I said. "I'm here because . . ." June's face and long hair flashed through my mind. I was blushing like crazy. "I'm here because adults at school wouldn't help Dominic even when he told them what was happening. And I want to know why. Or for that to change."

Tyler opened his mouth, but Zoe stopped him and pointed to the next girl.

The other two girls said stuff about safe places and support. Then Tyler jumped in.

"So what exactly happened with this Dominic kid? I mean, I've gotten pushed into a few lockers, and I stay away from certain people, but it sounds like he got it bad."

"I don't know a lot," I said. "I saw him getting . . . grabbed and kind of beat up in the hall and one of my teachers saw it too and didn't do anything. I know she heard the guy call Dominic a faggot. And the other guy, he was grabbing him . . ." I felt embarrassed.

"Grabbing his junk and saying he liked it?" asked Tyler. "Closet cases are the worst. They're like all over you because *they* like it. Cowards."

Emilio looked sick. I wondered if stuff like that had happened to him.

"And he told me he'd talked to one of the vice principals, and he just told him not to be so gay," I finished.

Everyone moaned. "I hate this school," said one of the girls.

Zoe looked grim. "There's something going on, but I can't get it out of Salazar. It's not just the GSA being denied. The teachers are totally freaked about anything having to do with gay people. We're not playing Copland for the next band concert, and I swear it's because he's gay."

I opened my mouth to tell them about Wellie and the Harlem Renaissance, but one of the girls spoke up first.

"Yeah and why has Salazar, like, gone back in the closet? My older sister had him, and he used to tell his classes about his partner and stuff, but now he never talks about that. And he doesn't have any pictures on his desk anymore, and I know he had some before."

"Maybe they broke up," said Tyler.

She shook her head. "I was with my family at the mall, and we saw him with a guy. My sister said that was his boyfriend. They've been together, like, ten years."

A janitor poked his head out of the door.

"You kids got permission to be out here? Unless you're here for a sport or with a teacher, you need to leave." He pointed a finger at Emilio, who was nervously eating chips. "And no food out here!"

CHAPTER 16

"We'll get together again soon!" Zoe called out as everyone split up. She fell into step with me. "Need a ride home?"

"Uh, OK," I said. The girl I thought was Zoe's girlfriend had disappeared. Zoe led me to her car in the parking lot.

"So, my mom wants to tell someone that no adult helped Dominic, but I told her she can't because then his parents would find out," I said as Zoe backed her car out.

"Yeah, the teachers and administrators not helping kids who are being bullied for being gay is the biggest problem," she said. "I mean, for some of us. Some of us don't get as much hassle, maybe just because we're more confident or whatever. But I worry about kids like Emilio and Nessa. I think they've had some problems."

Nessa must have been one of the girls at the meeting, I thought. "So does Mr. Salazar stand up for kids if they're called names?" I asked.

Zoe twisted her mouth like before. "I've seen him be a pansy about it." She stopped and snorted. "You know what I mean. He tells kids to knock it off, but he doesn't really address it. Not like I think he would if it were something else. Like calling someone—" she looked at me. "You know, a racist name or something. Where do you live again?"

When I was getting out of the car, Zoe leaned over to look at me. "Hey, if your mom is cool and like into PTA stuff, maybe you could ask her if there's something going on, something big. I think there's something the teachers and stuff are scared about. I'll ask my parents too. And the GSA will meet again, soon. Bye."

Before my mom got home, I spent some time thinking about what to tell her. She was into PTA stuff and did know a lot of people. I wasn't going to mention the GSA meeting, though. I wasn't sure why I didn't want to tell her about it.

I talked to her while she was making dinner so she was a little distracted.

"So I was talking to some other kids about Dominic being bullied," I said. "And it sounds like other kids have had problems and the teachers haven't really helped. And Matteo said all the gay people were missing from my Harlem Renaissance unit. And the band's not playing Aaron Copland. So do you think that there's like a thing about gay people in the school?"

Mom looked up from her recipe. "What? Honey, I'm confused." She turned to the cupboard. "Two tablespoons," she muttered.

"Like maybe it's the principal who hates gay people and all the teachers and administrators know that," I said.

My mom looked skeptical. "Even if that were true, the principal can't . . . there are policies about bullying and what has to be covered in the curriculum . . ."

She looked thoughtful for a moment. "But there was that group of parents last year who were really vocal about something at the school having to do with . . . homosexuality. A club?"

"The GSA?" I said, my throat tightening. Mom raised her eyebrows. "Gay Straight Alliance," I said.

"Like a support group for those kids?" she asked, her brow furrowed.

"Kinda," I shrugged.

"Hmm," she tapped her cookbook.

"Could you find out more? Like talk to some other parents or PTA people?" I asked.

She looked at me. I could see her thinking *Why are you so interested?* But then she thought of Dominic, and somehow that was an explanation. She nodded.

"There's a PTA meeting next week—you could come."

I was horrified. "Kids don't go to those, do they?"

"They can." She grabbed a paper calendar off her desk. "And there's a school board meeting two weeks after that if you were interested."

I shook my head. "I don't—can't you just ask around? I'm just wondering if something's going on that explains . . . stuff."

"And if there is?" she asked, her head tilted.

I shrugged again. "We'll see."

After dinner, Mom said, "I think I remember there were some letters to the editor from the parents involved in the club thing. But I didn't really pay attention because it wasn't something you or Matteo . . ." she trailed off.

"Thanks," I said, escaping to my room.

It took some searching, but I finally did find one letter that I thought was what she was talking about. It was from last year, and it was signed Sheila Walton. Cory Walton had been a senior last year and her sister, Shana, was in my class. Maybe this was their mom?

"GSAs encourage a sexual disorder," the letter said. "Vulnerable children are trained in these sex clubs to experiment with unhealthy behavior. Wake up, parents. If you don't want your child targeted to become part of the homosexual agenda, you need to oppose these clubs being allowed in our schools. It's for the safety of all our students."

That made my blood boil. Not allowing GSAs *protected* students? That was the stupidest thing I'd heard. It hadn't protected Dominic.

CHAPTER 17

"So?" I said, meeting Mom when she came in the door from the PTA meeting. She looked surprised to see me.

I'd seen Zoe and the others in the hallways a few times, but the GSA hadn't met again.

Dominic's funeral had been exactly as I expected. A few people from school were there. Mom and Papi both cried through the whole thing. I cried too, but I also felt mad at Dominic's poor parents. If they had seemed more accepting, wouldn't things be different? What did they think was Dominic's reason for killing himself? But for that matter, did I really know?

"Hi," said Mom. "Let me get in the door." She fussed around with her folders as I hovered.

"OK, I didn't find out a lot. I don't know exactly how different people feel on this topic so I have to be kind of careful. And there's not a natural opening to talk about it since you didn't want me to say anything about Dominic."

I bounced with impatience.

"But it does sound like when some kids tried to start that club—"

"The GSA," I interjected. Club sounded too much like Mrs. Walton's letter about sex clubs.

"Yes, that a group formed called the Concerned Parents, and they went to the school board."

"Yeah, and?"

"And I don't know what happened after that."

I turned away disappointed.

"But I do know that the minutes from the school board meetings are online," said Mom. "I get them in e-mails too, but I don't save them."

"Minutes are like the report of the meeting?"

"Yes, it's the record of what happened at the meeting. Pretty boring usually." Mom yawned. Then she looked at me. "You'll let me know what you're planning, right?"

For some reason, it made me defensive. "I thought you wanted to do something!" I said.

"I do," she said thoughtfully. "But . . . I just want to know what you're up to."

I huffed off to my room.

When I found the website, I started looking in the agenda and minutes documents around the date of Mrs. Walton's letter. Mom was right. It was super boring. Teacher retirements, student expulsions, lots of money stuff.

Then I found it.

"A proposed curriculum policy addressing sexual orientation."

Then stuff from the district attorney about nondiscrimination.

Then Mrs. Walton's name jumped out at me.

"Teaching about sexual matters, including homosexuality, is best left to families and churches," the minutes reported she said. Then someone from a group who "promotes the equality of gay, lesbian, bisexual, and transgender people" spoke. She said the policy would make it impossible for teachers and staff to talk about anything having to do with gay and lesbian people without permission from the superintendent.

What?! I thought. That is so weird. The minutes said they'd discuss the new policy at the next meeting.

I waited impatiently for the PDF of the next meeting to download. I scrolled through all the junk in the beginning with the calendar and stuff.

I read: "The new policy applies not only to the health curriculum but to all curriculum areas. The proposed policy is to create a safe working and learning environment for both staff and students in compliance with State and Federal laws. Its focus is respect and tolerance."

"Motion for the new policy... Seconded..."

And that was it. Did that mean that they had said yes to the policy? And what did it say?

I kept looking and in all the junk at the bottom (rental agreements and laundry contracts—who knew), I found the policy.

I charged into my parents' room with my laptop. They were both reading in bed.

"Staff shall remain unbiased on matters regarding sexual orientation...." my mom read out loud. "What is this, Isabel?"

"The policy," I said, pacing around the room. "The reason teachers and administrators won't help kids like Dominic."

"Are you sure this is it? Did you see if it was approved?"

I showed her the part about the motion and the seconded. "Is that what this means?" I asked. She nodded. "Yes, looks like it. Honey—" she reached out a hand to me. "I'm really tired. Can we talk about this more tomorrow? I'm not sure your take on this is right." I frowned. "Give us kisses and go to bed."

Reluctantly I did.

CHAPTER 18

At breakfast my mom tried to convince me that "unbiased" was a good thing. I had printed out some of the pages to show Zoe. I read to Mom what the GLBT woman had said about the policy making teachers unable to talk about homosexuality at all. She shook her head.

At lunch I found Zoe before going to sit with my friends.

"Here," I said sticking the pages out at her. "Read this and then maybe we can meet again soon?" She looked up, surprised. I hurried away, embarrassed for some reason.

The next day at lunch Zoe came up to me at our lunch table. My friends all eyed her.

"Thanks," Zoe said. "Thursday, OK? Meet in the parking lot."

"That was that girl again," said Jenny.

I nodded. I could tell they thought I was being weird about it. I didn't care.

On Thursday the parking lot was a zoo right after school. How was I supposed to find anyone? Then someone threw an arm around my shoulders.

"I spy with my little gay eye an ally!" yelled Tyler. He dropped his arm. "Where's Zoe? I hope we're going to Subway."

We found the others at Zoe's car.

"Shotgun!" Tyler yelled.

"I already called it," said one of the girls.

"My parents would kill me," said Zoe. "But you guys can cram into the backseat, right? It's only seven blocks." I tried to say I'd walk, but Tyler pushed me into the car.

"You can be in the middle and have my

butt," he said, shoving Emilio in next to me. The other girl got in the other side. Tyler crawled in and lay across our laps, humming.

"Everyone, buckle me in with you!" he insisted. We ignored him. We were so wedged in that I couldn't have reached my seat belt anyway.

At the coffee shop, Zoe filled everyone in on what I'd found. They all looked kind of baffled.

"But *unbiased* means 'not taking sides,'" one of the girls said. "Isn't that . . . good?"

Zoe smiled triumphantly. "I found out more. I got Salazar to crack when I showed him the policy. He admitted it has all the teachers scared. See, if you stand up for a kid who's being called a faggot, you're taking a side. You're saying it's OK to be gay and that people shouldn't be so stupid and prejudiced."

"Is this why my health teacher has yet to discuss safe sex for anyone other than vanilla heteros?" Tyler asked. Emilio blushed.

"And not talking about authors who were gay?" I added.

Zoe nodded. "It's so vague, and the administrators are so weird about it that none of the teachers know what's OK. So they feel safer saying nothing. Doesn't bother most of them," she said bitterly.

"But Salazar . . ." said one of the girls.

"He's afraid of losing his job," said Zoe. "He was pretty out to students and everyone before, but he's afraid he'll be targeted. And his partner is in grad school, and they're trying to adopt right now. . . ."

Tyler slurped his iced mocha. "So what do we do?"

"Well," Zoe said slowly. "We could say we think it's a bad policy. That it's hurting GLBT kids."

"Who's going to listen?" said Emilio.

"The school board," I said. "There's a meeting in two weeks. I think anyone can go." I stopped. What was I saying? I didn't want to go to a school board meeting. "Or maybe some parents could . . ." I trailed off.

Zoe's eyes lit up. "Great idea! I could totally get my mom to go and speak. But we need to have kids who are affected too, for the biggest impact."

Tyler elbowed me. "Thanks for volunteering all us queers."

"No one should talk who doesn't feel comfortable," said Zoe. "But maybe we can find a few people. . . ." she looked at us pleadingly. "There are other kids out there you know about—can we just try to talk to people?"

We all nodded.

"Then let's meet on Wednesday and see if you can bring anyone new along. We'll figure out then who's going to talk, OK? Bella, can you get us on the school board agenda?"

I nodded. I couldn't believe we were going to do this.

CHAPTER 19

Monday morning my mom was reading the paper at breakfast. I was just trying to wake up.

"How terrible," she murmured. I didn't pay much attention. But when she flipped the paper over to read the other page, I saw "teen suicide."

"What happened?" I asked, suddenly alert.

"A girl killed herself over the weekend. Not from your school but from one of the middle schools." Mom sighed.

"Was she gay?" I asked.

Mom looked at me over her glasses. "I'm not sure at that age. . . . It just says here that her family says she was being harassed for being a tomboy."

On my way to school, I stuffed the paper in my bag.

There was nothing on the morning announcements, but I guess since it wasn't our school, they didn't have to tell us anything. Kids could be killing themselves at other schools all over the district, and we'd never know.

At lunch I rushed up to Zoe.

"I heard," she said grimly. "That's my old middle school. My cousin goes there. I don't know why I didn't think of it before, but we should be reaching out to GSAs at other schools, especially for the school board meeting."

"There are GSAs at other schools?" I asked. We drifted over to a table and sat down to eat while we talked. Lunch was only twenty minutes after all.

"Some. There's one at that middle school. That's why I wanted one here. I didn't go to a meeting until eighth grade, but it helped me a lot. I'm going to talk to Ms. Klein—she's the GSA adviser there—after school and see if any of her students would come to the school board meeting. Wanna come?"

"Sure . . ." I said, glancing over at my friends. "I'm gonna go now. . . ."

Zoe nodded, not offended. "I'll meet you at my car."

Ms. Klein at the middle school was really happy to see Zoe but very emotional about Lydia, the girl who killed herself.

"She came to a couple of meetings, but she didn't say much. I think she was dating another girl in the group, but they broke up. Her parents are the ones who have come forward about the bullying. I guess they didn't know much until after her death. Her sister told them a little, and they looked through her text messages. . . . It was terrible the things other kids were saying to her." She stopped to wipe her eyes and blow her nose.

"I think her parents had tried to ignore her sexuality, or she hadn't told them much. But now they are outraged that she was being harassed and no one did anything." Ms. Klein continued.

"Did anyone know?" Zoe asked.

Ms. Klein nodded. "She showed some of the texts to the principal. She told her to change her number. Her sister had heard about that too."

Then Zoe asked her about the policy. Ms. Klein nodded.

"Teachers only heard about it from their principals. We can't find out what it means. And I've been pushing for years for staff training on how to handle bullying, especially when it's GLBT related."

She sighed.

"I don't know the best way to help either. There are plenty of other students who have come to me with suicidal thoughts or serious depression. I'm scared to refer them to the counselor—I've heard she's not very helpful. And honestly, many teachers are worried about their jobs."

We told her about the school board meeting and our plans.

"Do you think any of your students would come and talk about problems with bullying and adults in school not helping?" said Zoe.

Ms. Klein looked thoughtful. "Maybe. I'll ask. It would be amazing if we could get that policy changed. Maybe then I wouldn't be so desperate to find a job in another district." She cracked a little smile.

"I got in trouble for offering snacks when the GSA started. That Concerned Parents group said I was trying to lure kids into being gay. With Cheetos!" Ms. Klein shook her head. "I don't have snacks at meetings anymore."

"The Concerned Parents lady, Mrs. Walton, spoke at the meeting when the policy was passed," I said.

"They're a very formidable group," said Ms. Klein, looking nervous. "But I think you're right to take them on."

CHAPTER 20

And then it was the night of the school board meeting. There were four kids willing to talk and Lydia's parents.

It almost didn't happen. When I'd e-mailed to get on the agenda, I got a reply from the secretary saying that the policy wasn't "up for review" for two more years. "Exactly what do you want to say?" the secretary wrote.

At first, I was going to call Zoe. She'd given me her number, but I felt shy about it.

Then I had a better idea. I called Matteo.

He was really distracted at first, but when I yelled at him and cried a little, he started listening. I told him everything I could think of.

"Well, it sounds like there's a connection between the policy and bullying not being stopped. And some of this bullying may have led to the suicides." It was so simple when he said it like that.

So that's exactly what I wrote back to the secretary. She responded that we'd have fifteen minutes on the agenda.

When I got to the meeting with my mom, I saw Zoe right away with her parents. They were both wearing PFLAG T-shirts. Zoe was craning her neck to look for everyone else.

"We have to sign up to talk during "open discussion" on a topic. Other people I don't know are already signed up for our topic," she said in a low voice.

"Is one Mrs. Walton?" I asked.

"Yeah and a couple of others. I wasn't going to talk, but maybe I should sign up just to hold a spot? Or put down one of the others' names? I don't think the secretary would let me sign up everyone," Zoe gestured toward a sour looking woman in a pink sweater at the front table. Zoe chewed a hangnail until it bled.

"Oh, there's Ms. Klein with Lydia's parents!" Zoe ran over and took them up to the secretary.

They all came back to sit with us. Lydia's mom was wiping her eyes.

Ms. Klein leaned over to me. "Zoe said you might speak Spanish?"

I nodded hesitantly.

"Mr. and Mrs. Mendoza speak English of course, but they're really emotional. If they needed a little translating, could you help?"

"Uhh," I said. Then my mom leaned into the conversation.

"Of course we'll help." She went over to Mrs. Mendoza and put an arm around her as she talked. Mrs. Mendoza's tears really started flowing as she patted my mom's arm and nodded. Mom came back and sat next to me again.

"Um, thanks," I whispered to her. She squeezed my hand and got out a Kleenex.

Everyone showed up who said they'd speak. After Zoe got the last person signed up, she whispered, "Everyone's going to have two minutes or less. The secretary uses a stopwatch for the whole meeting."

Then one of the people up front banged that hammer thing, and the meeting started.

Our row was vibrating with nervousness through the whole boring beginning of the meeting.

Then, "Discussion of the curriculum policy regarding sexual orientation. This policy was passed by the board last school year. We invite those signed up to speak to the microphone. Please keep your comments brief. We have fifteen minutes for this portion of the meeting. Sheila Walton is the first on our list."

Mrs. Walton stepped up to the microphone. "May I go last instead?" she asked. The secretary nodded.

Next was another member of the Concerned Parents who just rambled about the importance of leaving discussions of "homosexual lifestyles" to parents and churches "where they belong." Another one said something similar. Then they called Lydia's parents.

My mom went up to the microphone with them, though they didn't end up needing her. Mostly they had a hard time speaking because they were crying so hard. Lydia's mom said they found almost a hundred texts calling Lydia a "dyke" and telling her she'd be "better off dead."

"And when she told the principal, she just told her to change her number. What kind of help is that? What do you think those kids were saying to her at school?" Mrs. Mendoza said, trying to take deep breaths.

"Time," said the secretary.

CHAPTER 21

A ll the kids talked next. They did OK, but the school board didn't do anything to make them less nervous. Some of the school board members barely looked interested or sympathetic. A couple of kids mumbled or talked too fast.

Couldn't the school board see that even to come and talk about these embarrassing things showed how serious it was? I thought. The whole thing was very frustrating.

Then the secretary called "Sheila Walton," again.

Mrs. Walton adjusted the microphone. "Some of the stories we've heard tonight are quite upsetting," she said. "However, I would like to remind everyone that the district already has a policy against bullying. Also, research shows that children who identify as gay have more mental health problems. This is why our group of Concerned Parents has opposed allowing the GSA clubs in our schools to promote such an unhealthy lifestyle." She held out a paper. "There are resources available to help individuals wishing to leave the homosexual lifestyle. I would like to see these resources available to all students who are struggling." Then she sat down.

My blood was pounding in my ears so hard I could barely hear. One of the school board members said something about "looking into" the matter. Then we had to sit through the rest of the boring meeting.

All I could think about was how Mrs. Walton had said the Lydia and Dominic had killed themselves because they were gay. Which was true in a way, but not how she meant it.

"Look," said my mom the next day. "We're famous." She showed me the newspaper. There was a photo of the Mendozas at the microphone with my mom sitting nearby. And a short description of the comments at the meeting.

"Students and parents claim that the district policy is contributing to bullying of GLBT students, some of whom have committed suicide in the past two years," the paper said. Well, at least someone seemed to have gotten it.

I don't think any of us wanted to admit it, but the school board meeting had felt so scary that no one really wanted to go to the next one to find out if they were going to do anything.

"Whatever they say will be in the minutes," Zoe said. The GSA was sitting in Salazar's room. I think he was embarrassed he wasn't doing more so he had told Zoe we could start using his room to meet.

"My mom gets the e-mail and they put them online," I said. "I'll let everyone know."

"I'm not holding my breath," said Tyler. "Now, I think we need a chant to cheer us up. Hands in! GSA! GSA!" We rolled our eyes, but soon we were laughing and getting loud.

So loud we didn't notice Shana Walton standing in the doorway until Mr. Salazar yelled, "Guys!" as he went over to talk to her. We hushed immediately. Shana had some question about auditions for the next play.

Mr. Salazar didn't say anything when she left, just went back to his desk to keep grading, but his face was set.

"I hope we didn't get him in trouble," I said to Zoe as we left. She looked worried too.

CHAPTER 22

I thought the minutes would come out right after the next meeting, but it took a few days. I called Zoe as soon as I saw them.

"The school board has determined that none of the suicides were related to episodes of bullying or harassment," I read to her.

"What?!" she screamed into the phone.

"The policy does not need review at this time," I continued. "That's it. That's all it says."

"Ugh," she said. "I didn't think they were

going to be super helpful, but this is worse. It's—it's just saying it never happened! Oh, God."

She was quiet for a minute. "Well, there's nothing that should really prevent the GSA from being official since other schools have them. I guess that's what we should focus on now. So at least there's a safe place." She sounded really sad.

CHAPTER 23

At the next meeting, Zoe asked Salazar again why we hadn't been approved.

"The proposal has been sitting on Mrs. Rice's desk for months. Mrs. Carney was supposed to be the GSA adviser, but she was transferred. She asked me to do it."

Salazar looked down at his hands.

"Mrs. Rice asked me to take 'gay' out of the name," he said, and eveyone snorted.

"I said no, GSA was the name used in most

schools, including others in the district. Then she wanted permission slips from parents."

Emilio blanched.

"Obviously that's a no-go too—lots of kids aren't out to their parents. And other student organizations aren't required to do that. And now she's just sitting on it," Salazar finished.

"When," Zoe said carefully, "did you last ask her about it?"

Salazar sighed. "Months ago. I'll ask again, I promise. You guys are being brave—I need to be too, even if . . ." We all looked away. Tyler changed the subject.

We met again a few days later because Salazar had news.

"Good news," he said. "The principal approved the GSA once I hinted that there could be legal problems if she didn't."

Everyone cheered.

"Less good news," he said. "I can't be the adviser. . . ." Everyone looked shocked. "The principal heard that we were meeting on school property without permission. She's appointed a counselor, Ms. Lopez, to be the adviser."

"But can she do that?" asked Zoe angrily. "Just decide who the adviser will be?"

Salazar nodded. "Any kind of after-school thing means extra pay for the staff person, so they always have to be approved. And she also said she thought a counselor was more appropriate given the 'psychological needs' of students in the GSA."

Everyone started talking angrily at once. Salazar waved his hands.

"I'm really sorry," he said, "but I have to ask you to leave. I'll get written up if there are more unofficial meetings. You'll have to talk to Ms. Lopez about the next meeting."

We all turned to go. As we trickled into the hallway, Salazar called out, "You're always welcome to come talk to me. Anytime!"

Before we split up, Zoe said she'd talk to Lopez. She turned to me, frowning. "I've got some errands. Otherwise, I'd offer you a ride."

"No problem," I murmured.

It felt like failure all around. The bad policy was still there. The GSA might turn out to be a joke depending on what Ms. Lopez was like. I trudged home.

CHAPTER 24

The newspaper had only a paragraph after the school board said it saw no connection between the suicides and bullying. I don't think anyone except us noticed it.

Then everything changed.

This time my mom had the paper open at my spot at the table when I came down for breakfast. On the front page of the local section the headlines read, "Another student suicide. Is district policy to blame?"

It was a kid from another high school, but the details were all too familiar. Bullying "related to sexual orientation" the paper said. Friends claimed that teachers had been aware of the bullying but hadn't done much.

"Sometimes they'd say, 'that's inappropriate,'" said one girl they interviewed. "But they never really stepped in and to help Luke."

"The school board could not be reached for comment," the article concluded.

There was a little box too about "suicide epidemics" and whether it was true that suicide was catching, like a cold.

At school, people were buzzing about it. It had been going on right under everyone's nose, but now people were noticing.

I said this to Zoe at lunch. She nodded.

"My parents know Luke's parents through PFLAG," she said.

"Uh, maybe I should know this," I interrupted, "but what is PFLAG?"

"Parents, Families, and Friends of Lesbians and Gays," said Zoe. "Sometimes my parents are a little too into it, you know? Like they want to participate in every part of your life because they think that will keep you from separating from them or something? Anyway, this guy, Luke, his parents are lawyers."

I just looked at her, confused.

"They might get more from the school board than we did," she said.

"Ohhhh," I said. Nobody really knew what might happen with lawyers involved, so we focused on the GSA.

"Did you talk to Lopez?" I asked.

"Yeah, twice," sighed Zoe. "She said she's totally busy. Lots of students are showing up in her office and parents are calling her about their kids cutting and stuff like that."

Suicide epidemic, I thought.

"I pointed out that the GSA could support people who feel desperate. At any rate, if she doesn't make time for it soon, we could ask the principal for an adviser who actually has time to meet," Zoe said fiercely. I nodded, not sure I would be brave enough to do that.

CHAPTER 25

I went to join my friends at our lunch table after talking to Zoe. They hadn't really said anything about it, but they also were always in the middle of some big conversation when I sat down. Usually I just listened and then lunch was over. Simple. But today Jenny turned to me.

"Um, Bella, this is going to sound weird, but are you OK? I mean, I just feel like you've been kind of distant lately. Withdrawal from friends is one of the signs . . . " she said, tears in her eyes.

Keesha was watching me, but Kim kept eating like nothing was happening.

Before I could say anything, Jenny continued. "With all this going on, I just, you know, feel like every time I say good-bye to someone that I don't know if I'll see them again." She started to sob. Keesha put her arm around her. Kim put down her spoon to hold Jenny's hand.

Part of me wanted to roll my eyes, but these were my friends. I *had* been pulling away, and maybe it was time to stop. And I got what Jenny was saying. A lot of people our age were killing themselves. It did make you look around and wonder *who's next?*

"No, Jenny, I'm OK. Really," I said softly. "But I'm sorry if it seems like I've been blowing you guys off lately." I took a deep breath. "The thing is, I've been helping that girl, Zoe, try to start a GSA for our school. And we went with a bunch of other kids to a school board meeting to talk about the policy and why it's bad."

I paused.

"Why didn't you tell us?" said Kim, looking me in the eye.

I blushed. "I guess, I wasn't sure how you'd feel about it. Or what you might think. . . ."

Keesha jumped in. "We're not prejudiced, you know," she said angrily. "But does this mean there's something else you need to tell us too?"

I shook my head, not really getting what she was asking or, at least, not wanting to get it.

At the same time, Kim said, "Keesha, it's a gay-*straight* alliance—anyone can join. Sounds like something we need at this school and every school. I don't know why the school board has their heads so far up their butts to think that something like that would be a problem. Seems better than kids killing themselves."

Everyone nodded. Then the bell rang.

CHAPTER 26

Zoe finally got a date from Ms. Lopez. It was kind of last minute, but the six of us were there in the library, waiting, when Ms. Lopez rushed in.

"Sorry, sorry, I had a student appointment that ran over," she said. She looked tired. And annoyed.

"So, is there anything you need to do?" Zoe asked Lopez. Lopez looked confused. "Like, to make this an official meeting?" Zoe was trying to be polite, but she sounded a little snarky.

Ms. Lopez sighed. "No, I'm just here because every student club has to have a faculty adviser. But if you'd like me to facilitate and get the ball rolling, I'm happy to. Does anyone have a joy or concern to share?"

She got a lot of blank stares. Then Zoe said, "I thought we could talk about plans to get the word out about the GSA now that it's official, I mean, now that it exists."

"Posters, goody," said Tyler, pulling some markers out of his bag. "I've been practicing my bubble letters just in case."

"Yeah, in a minute," said Zoe. "But we also need to talk to someone on the school newspaper. And can we set a time for the next meeting so we can put it on the posters and get it in the morning announcements?" She looked at Lopez.

"I'll check my calendar while you work on posters," Ms. Lopez muttered.

Tyler grabbed some paper out of the printer. "I'll go charm some bigger stuff out of the art teacher," he said. "Start with this."

We came up with a list of slogans to use and got going.

You're not alone, I wrote, trying to get it to space evenly. Emilio was drawing rainbows in every corner of his paper.

Lopez came back and said she could meet again in two weeks.

"I'm just really booked after school—a lot of students are hurting," she said, self-importantly.

"Sometimes it helps to have something positive to do," Zoe said, not looking up as she wrote *Gay? Lesbian? Bi? Transgender? Queer? Questioning?* on her poster. "I thought maybe as a group we could go to the rally for marriage equality next Friday night. We could make some posters about that too and meet at school to carpool."

Lopez eyed Zoe's poster like she wanted to say something about it.

"Of course any of you can go to this rally on your own, with your parents," she said smoothly. "I'm not sure as a school-related. . . . I don't think it's a topic that is of great concern to many people your age. I don't think many are thinking about *marriage* yet!" She laughed loudly.

Zoe's mouth dropped open. Then she narrowed her eyes. "Gosh," she said sarcastically, "I guess when you were our age it wouldn't have bothered you at all to know that you might never be able to get married in the same way as everyone else."

Lopez flushed and looked angry.

"I'm going if anyone needs a ride," said Zoe, turning back to her poster. She drew two little stick girls with their arms around each other.

"Going to what?" Tyler asked as he breezed in with big sheets of paper. "Oh, the rally? I'm getting a ride from June, so I'll see you there."

"June?" I whipped my head around fast.

"Yeah, June with the super long hair, you know? Her mom's a lesbo." Zoe shot him a look. "What? We need to take back the language, make it ours," said Tyler. He tapped

Zoe's poster. "See, like 'queer'—used to be an insult. Go ahead, call me a—"

"Let's try to keep our language appropriate for school," interrupted Lopez. "Some people find those terms offensive." Then she buried her nose in paperwork and barely looked up when we went to hang up the posters in the halls.

CHAPTER 27

I told Zoe I wanted to go to the rally. And I decided I had to mention it to my friends. None of them said they wanted to come, but they seemed to have accepted that this was my *thing* now.

We did see Tyler and June at the rally for a minute. June looked a little surprised to see me. Then we got separated in the crowd. The rally was exciting—I'd never been to anything like that. Zoe and I were both hoarse from screaming afterward.

June came up to me on Monday at my locker. My heart pounded like always around her.

"Tyler said you went to that school board meeting?" she said. I nodded. "Did you hear that Luke's parents are suing the district about the policy?"

So that's how everything changed.

Luke's parents heard about the school board meeting when parents and kids tried to explain how bad it was. They took that and Luke's experiences and went to one of those big organizations that sue when people's rights aren't being protected.

Because I had never heard of this (or paid attention, more likely), Matteo tried to explain to me how important these groups are. I guess they're pretty important.

By the GSA meeting later in the week, Zoe had lots more details. There were a few new kids so we started with introductions. Lopez seemed ready to make some other "ice breaker" comment or speech, but Zoe jumped in.

"I have really important news," she said, grinning. "Luke—he was the last kid in the district who killed himself—his parents are part of a lawsuit against the district. Along with Lydia Mendoza's parents. The lawsuit says that the policy makes teachers discriminate against kids for their sexual orientation and allows violence to happen."

Zoe passed around the minutes from the meeting with the policy highlighted.

"Staff shall remain unbiased," I read again. How weird that something so simple could cause so much pain. It didn't even sound evil.

"So they're going to have a trial?" one of the new kids asked. I was picturing that too.

"No," Zoe said, "the district is already trying to settle. Shell out some money to make it stop. But they also won't admit the policy is wrong or causing all these problems." She shook her head. *"Problems* doesn't seem like the right word when kids are being tortured and killing themselves."

"Torture's a good word," said Nessa quietly. "Sometimes I feel like a prisoner in the torture

chamber called school. Only no one touches me—they just use words."

"And how does that make you feel?" asked Lopez. Everyone ignored her. We gave Nessa a group hug.

"Sounds like you should be suing the district," said Tyler.

"Maybe," said Nessa and bit her lip.

CHAPTER 28

I tried to keep an eye out for Nessa after that. She was one of those little freshman girls whom you normally didn't notice as they scurried past. A week later I saw Zoe chatting with her by her locker. Zoe waved me over.

"Guess what?! She did it. She really did! Nessa has some balls—I mean ovaries!" Zoe jumped up and down.

"Whaaat?" I said.

"I joined the lawsuit," Nessa said,

grinning. "I thought, Zoe's right, it helps to do something to fight back. So I looked up their number and I called Luke's parents at work and they told me more about it and then they talked to my parents." That was the most I'd ever heard her say.

"And your parents?" I asked.

"Well, they kind of knew some of what was going on. And after talking to Luke's parents . . . I mean, it kind of scared them. They're not bad. I just hadn't told them because I wasn't sure if they could handle it. They had a kind of 'don't ask, don't tell' attitude."

"But we know what happened to DADT!" Zoe crowed, pulling out her phone and flashing at us the famous picture of the navy woman kissing her girlfriend. Nessa grinned again and flipped open her locker to show us the same picture torn out of a magazine and taped inside her door.

At the next GSA meeting, Zoe had an update.

"The school board still says the policy is

fine, but it's on the agenda to be discussed at the next meeting. The lawyers said that the district must be changing the language. Or maybe getting rid of it! I'm going—does anyone else want to come?"

"It's a *school* board meeting," said Zoe, looking at Lopez. "We should definitely be able to go as a GSA, not just on our own. And put it on the morning announcements so other people can come with us. It's *educational*."

We all held our breath. Lopez looked defeated. She shrugged and said "OK."

CHAPTER 29

The meeting was packed. Nessa sat up front with the lawyers and the Mendozas and Luke's parents.

Everyone was impatient as the school board moved through all the boring stuff in the beginning. Then, "the school board proposes new language for the curriculum policy addressing sexual orientation. The board proposes that the policy now read: 'Teachers and staff shall not share their personal opinions about inflammatory topics in the course of their school-related duties.' Now we have a very short time for discussion."

Mrs. Walton was the first to talk. "Making any changes to this policy at all is just giving in to the gay activists in our schools. It encourages them to continue to try to recruit our children using these homosexual clubs," she said.

I wondered what reality she was living in. Did she even know what a GSA was?

Then one of the lawyers for our side spoke next. "Obviously 'inflammatory topics' means anything having to do with GLBT people. This policy discourages any classroom discussion about history, literature, science, current events, or any other relevant lessons involving GLBT people. The policy tells all students that GLBT people are too disgusting to be talked about inside the school walls. How do you think that affects GLBT students? Unfortunately, we've already seen the results," he said, gesturing to the Mendozas and Lydia's parents.

It was quiet for a moment, and then someone began to slowly clap.

"Discussion closed," the secretary snapped into the microphone. "Fifteen-minute recess for the board to discuss."

The school board all got up and went out another door. The room buzzed. Then they were back.

"Slightly different language is suggested," said the secretary. She read, "Teachers will not try to convince students to agree or disagree with any particular opinion with respect to these issues. When discussing these issues, district staff will uphold the dignity and self-worth of all students, regardless of their race, color, creed, religion, national origin, sex/gender, disability, status with regard to public assistance, sexual orientation, or age."

Was that better? I wondered. It sounded a little better.

"Further decisions about the policy will be announced at a future meeting," another school board member said. And then it was over.

CHAPTER 30

"How was it?" my mom asked when I got home. "Sorry I wasn't able to go."

I filled her in.

"You seem sad," she said. "But look how far things have come. It may take a while with a lawsuit dragging out, but something's definitely going to happen."

I shrugged. "I know. . . . It's just that it doesn't feel like we made anything change. It's all the lawyers threatening them. The school board blew us off the first time. And our GSA kind of sucks because of Ms. Lopez."

"Yes, but without all of you speaking up, Luke's parents might not have known that this was happening everywhere to other kids. You set something in motion. I'm proud of you," Mom said.

My eyes filled with tears. I still wasn't sure how my parents felt about all this. Sometimes I didn't know how I felt either.

"Would you guys . . . I mean, I know you love me no matter what, but what if I were gay or something?" I asked.

My mom looked at me over her reading glasses and elbowed my dad who was sitting next to her on the couch. "Kiko, our daughter is talking to us. Turn off the TV."

"Hmm?" said Papi as he held out the remote to zap the TV.

"Of course we would always love you," Mom said. "Nothing could change that."

"Nada, nada, nada," said Papi, holding out his arms to me. He hugged me close. I decided just to leave it there and snuggle in against him.

CHAPTER 31

The news we heard about the school board was kind of ho-hum when it came. They settled the lawsuit and kept the changed language about not convincing students and "affirming dignity." No one was sure if that would make a big difference.

Then we got better news.

"Ms. Lopez asked the principal to find another adviser for the GSA due to her busy schedule," Salazar told us, beaming. "And when it came up at the staff meeting, no one else volunteered except me." We all cheered.

"And the next staff meeting will be trainings to help teachers learn how to deal with bullying, especially bullying of GLBT kids or kids who others think might be gay," he told us. "All the district schools have to do these trainings, and I get to help organize it."

"About time," said Zoe dryly.

"Finally, GSAs were specifically mentioned at the last school board meeting as being allowed in all district middle and high schools," Salazar finished.

"I bet Mrs. Walton didn't like that," I said.

"There was pushback, but it's so cut-and-dry legally that after the lawsuit they had to make it clear that principals can't block GSAs from forming," Salazar said.

Everyone agreed that was good. Then we started talking about Mid-Winter Festival and whether it would be a good or bad thing to try to nominate Tyler for queen.

Afterward, Zoe offered me a ride.

"I kind of feel let down," she said. "I

thought it was going to be a big fight that we could win. Now we know we kind of won, hopefully things will get better, but it wasn't really us. It was the threat of lawsuits, not because they saw how right we were."

I told her what my mom had said about setting something in motion.

"Yeah, my mom said something like that too," said Zoe, chewing her lip. "I guess this is just how these things go in the real world. It's not like a fight at recess that you win or lose."

She pulled into my driveway. When I got out, Zoe leaned over to look at me. "Oh, I meant to tell you—June said she thinks you're really interesting." She smirked at me and threw the car into reverse.

About the Author

Elizabeth Karre is a writer and editor living in St. Paul, MN.

SOUTHSIDE HIGH

ARE YOU A SURVIVOR?

The Alliance

Bad Deal

Beaten

Benito Runs

Dance Team

Deadly Drive

The Fight

Full Impact

Overexposed

Plan B

Recruited

Shattered Star

check out all the books in the

SURVIVING SOUTH SIDE

collection